FLAT STANLEY

Stanley's Christmas Adventure

**DON'T MISS ANY OF THESE
OUTRAGEOUS STORIES:**

Flat Stanley: His Original Adventure!
Stanley and the Magic Lamp
Invisible Stanley
Stanley's Christmas Adventure
Stanley in Space
Stanley, Flat Again!

**AND CATCH FLAT STANLEY'S
WORLDWIDE ADVENTURES:**

The Mount Rushmore Calamity
The Great Egyptian Grave Robbery
The Japanese Ninja Surprise
The Intrepid Canadian Expedition
The Amazing Mexican Secret

FLAT STANLEY

Stanley's Christmas Adventure

by Jeff Brown
Pictures by Macky Pamintuan

HARPER
An Imprint of HarperCollinsPublishers

FOR DUNCAN

Stanley's Christmas Adventure
Text copyright © 1993 by Jeff Brown
Illustrations by Macky Pamintuan, copyright © 2010 by HarperCollins Publishers.
All rights reserved. Printed in the United States of America. No part of this
book may be used or reproduced in any manner whatsoever without written
permission except in the case of brief quotations embodied in critical articles and
reviews. For information address HarperCollins Children's Books, a division of
HarperCollins Publishers, 10 East 53rd Street, New York, NY 10022.
www.harpercollinschildrens.com

Library of Congress catalog card number: 2010921893
ISBN 978-0-06-442175-1

Typography by Alison Klapthor
10 11 12 13 14 15   CG/CW   10 9 8 7 6 5 4 3 2 1
❖
First US paperback edition, 2003
Reillustrated edition, 2010
First published in Great Britain 1993 by Methuen
Children's Books Ltd.

CONTENTS

Prologue

She was the sort of little girl who liked to be *sure* of things, so she went all over Snow City, checking up.

The elves had done their work.

At the Post Office, Mail Elves had read the letters, making lists of who wanted what.

In the great workshops—the Doll

Room, the Toy Plant, the Game Mill—
Gift Elves had filled the orders, taking
care as to color and size and style.

In the Wrap Shed the gifts lay ready,
wrapped now in gay paper with holly
and pine cones, sorted by country, by
city or village, by road or lane or street.

The Wrap Elves teased her. "Don't
trust us, eh? . . . Snooping, we call
this, Miss!"

"Pooh!" said the little girl. "Well
done, elves! Good work!"

But at home in Snow City

Square, all was not well.

"Don't slam the door, dear," said her mother, weeping. "Your father's having his nap."

"Mother! What's wrong?"

"He won't go this year, he says!" The mother sobbed. "He's been so cross lately, but I never—"

"*Why? Why* won't he go?"

"They've lost faith, don't care anymore, he says! Surely not *everyone*, I said. Think of your favorite letter, the one by your desk! He just growled at me!"

"Pooh!" said the girl. "It's not fair! Really! I mean, everything's *ready*! Why—"

"Not now, dear," said the mother.

"It's been a dreadful day."

In the little office at the back of the house, the girl studied the letter her mother had mentioned, framed with others on a wall:

I am a regular boy, except that I got flat, the letter said. From an accident. I was going to ask for new clothes, but my mother already bought them. She had to, because of the flatness. So I'm just writing to say don't bother about me. Have a nice holiday. My father says be careful driving, there are lots of bad drivers this time of year.

The girl thought for a moment, and an idea came to her. "Hmmmm . . .

Well, why *not*?" she said.

She looked again at the letter.

The name LAMBCHOP was printed across the top, and an address. It was signed "Stanley, U.S.A."

Sarah

It was two nights before Christmas, and all through the house not a Lambchop was stirring, but something was.

Stanley Lambchop sat up in his bed. "Listen! Someone said 'Rat.'"

"It was more like 'grat,'" said his younger brother, Arthur, from his bed. "In the living room, I think."

The brothers tiptoed down the stairs.

For a moment all was silence in the darkened living room. Then came a *thump*. "Ouch!" said a small voice. "Drat again!"

"Are you a burglar?" Arthur called. "Did you hurt yourself?"

"I am *not* a burglar!" said the voice. "Where's the—Ah!" The lights came on.

The brothers stared.

Before the fireplace, by the Christmas tree, stood a slender, dark-haired little girl wearing a red jacket and skirt, both trimmed with white fur.

"I banged it *twice*," she said, rubbing her knee. "Coming down the chimney, and just now."

"We *do* have a front door, you know," said Stanley.

"Well, so does my house. But, you know, this time of year . . . ?" The girl sounded a bit nervous. "Actually, I've never done this before. Let's see . . . Ha, ha, ha! Season's Greetings! Ha, ha, ha!"

"'Ha, ha!' to you," said Arthur. "What's so funny?"

"Funny?" said the girl. "Oh! 'Ho, ho, ho!' I meant. I'm Sarah Christmas. Who are you?"

"Arthur Lambchop," said Arthur. "That's my brother, Stanley."

"It is? But he's not *flat*."

"He was, but I blew him up," Arthur explained. "With a bicycle pump."

"Oh, no! I wish you hadn't." Sarah Christmas sank into a chair. "Drat! It's all going wrong! Perhaps I shouldn't have come. But that's how I am.

Headstrong, my mother says. She—"

"Excuse me," Stanley said. "But where are you from?"

"And why *did* you come?" said Arthur.

Sarah told them.

Mr. and Mrs. Lambchop were reading in bed.

A tap came at the door, and then Stanley's voice. "Hey! Can I come in?"

Mr. and Mrs. Lambchop cared greatly for proper speech. "Hay is for horses, Stanley," she said. "And not 'can,' dear. You *may* come in."

Stanley came in.

"What is the explanation, my boy,

of this late call?" said Mr. Lambchop, remembering past surprises. "You have not, I see, become flat again. Has a genie come to visit? Or perhaps the President of the United States has called?"

Mrs. Lambchop smiled. "You are very amusing, George."

"Arthur and I were in bed," said Stanley. "But we heard a noise and went to see. It was a girl called Sarah Christmas, from Snow City. She talks a lot. She says her father says he won't come this year, but Sarah thinks he might change his mind if I ask him to. Because I wrote him a letter once that he liked. She wants me to go with her to Snow City. In her father's sleigh. It's at the North Pole, I think." Stanley caught his breath. "I said I'd have to ask you first."

"Quite right," said Mrs. Lambchop.

Mr. Lambchop went to the bathroom and drank a glass of water to calm himself.

"Now then, Stanley," he said, returning. "You have greatly startled us. Surely—"

"Put on your robe, George," said Mrs. Lambchop. "Let us hear for ourselves what this visitor has to say."

"This is *delicious*!" Sarah Christmas sipped the hot chocolate Mrs. Lambchop had served them all. "My mother makes it too, with cinnamon in it. And little cookies with—" Her glance had fallen on the mantelpiece. "What's *that*, pinned up there?"

"Christmas stockings," Stanley said. "The blue one's mine."

"But the other, the great square thing?"

"It's a pillowcase." Arthur blushed.

"My stocking wouldn't do. I have very small feet."

"Pooh!" Sarah laughed. "You wanted extra gifts, so—"

"Sarah, dear," Mrs. Lambchop said. "Your father? Has he truly made up his mind, you think?"

"Oh, yes!" Sarah sighed. "But I thought—Stanley being flat, that *really* interested him. I mean, I couldn't be *sure*, but if nobody ever did anything without—"

"You seem a very nice girl, Sarah." Mr. Lambchop gave a little laugh. "But you *have* been joking with us, surely? I—"

The phone rang, and he answered it.

"Hello, George," the caller said. "This is your neighbor, Frank Smith. I know it's late, but I must congratulate you on your Christmas lawn display! Best—"

"Lawn?" said Mr. Lambchop. "Display?"

"The sleigh! And those lifelike *reindeer*! What makes them move about like that? Batteries, I suppose?"

"Just a moment, Frank." Mr. Lambchop went to the window and looked out, Mrs.

Lambchop beside him.

"My goodness!" she said. "One, two, three, four . . . Eight! And such a pretty sleigh!"

Mr. Lambchop returned to the phone. "They *are* lifelike, aren't they? Goodbye. Thank you for calling, Frank."

"See? I'm not a joking kind of person, actually," said Sarah Christmas. "Now! My idea *might* work, even without the flatness. Do let Stanley go!"

"To the North Pole?" said Mrs. Lambchop. "At night? By himself? Good gracious, Sarah!"

"It's not fair, asking Stanley, but not me," said Arthur, feeling hurt. "It's always like this! I never—"

"Oh, pooh!" Sarah Christmas smiled. "Actually . . . You could *all* go. It's a very big sleigh."

Mr. and Mrs. Lambchop looked at each other, then at Stanley and Arthur, then at each other again.

"Stanley just might make a difference, George," Mrs. Lambchop said. "And if we can *all* go . . . ?"

"Quite right," said Mr. Lambchop. "Sarah, we will accompany you to Snow City!"

"Hooray!" shouted Stanley and Arthur, and Sarah too.

Mrs. Lambchop thought they should wait until Frank Smith had gone to bed. "Imagine the gossip," she said, "were he to see our reindeer fly away."

Mr. Lambchop called his office to leave a message on the nighttime answering machine. He would not be in tomorrow, he said, as he had been called unexpectedly out of town.

"There!" cried Stanley, by the window. "The Smiths' light is out."

The Lambchops changed quickly from pajamas to warmer clothing, and followed Sarah to the sleigh.

The Sleigh

"Welcome aboard!" said Sarah, from the driver's seat.

The Lambchops, sitting on little benches that made the big sleigh resemble a roofless bus, could scarcely contain their excitement.

The night sky shone bright with

stars, and from the windows of nearby houses red and green Christmas lights twinkled over snowy lawns and streets. Before them, the eight reindeer, fur shiny in the moonlight, tossed their antlered heads.

"Ready when you are, Sarah," Mr. Lambchop said.

"Good!" Sarah cleared her throat. "Fasten your seat belts, please! We are about to depart for Snow City. My name is Sarah—I guess you know that—and I'll be glad to answer any questions you may have. Please do not move about without permission of the Sleigh Master—that's me, at least right now—and obey whatever

instructions may—"

"Pu-leeese!" said Arthur.

"Oh, all right!" The Lambchops fastened their seat belts, and Sarah took up the reins. "Ready, One? Ready, Two, Three—"

"Just *numbers*?" cried Mrs. Lambchop. "Why, we know such lovely reindeer names! Dasher, Dancer, Prancer, Vixen—"

"Comet, Cupid, Donder, Blitzen!" shouted Arthur. "They're from a poem we know!"

"Those *are* good names!" said Sarah. "Ready, One through Eight?"

The reindeer pawed the ground, jingling their harness bells.

"Now!" said Sarah.

The jingling stopped suddenly, and a great silence fell.

Now a silver mist rose, swirling, about the sleigh. The startled Lambchops could see nothing beyond the mist, not their house nor the houses of their neighbors, not the twinkling Christmas lights, not the bright stars above. There was only the silver mist, everywhere, cool against their cheeks.

"What is this, Sarah?" Mrs. Lamb-chop called. "Are we not to proceed to Snow City?"

Sarah's voice came cheerfully through the mist. "We have proceeded. We're there!"

3

Snow City

Beyond the mist, excited voices rose. "Sarah's back! . . . With strangers! Big ones! . . . Where's she been?"

"Poppa's elves," said Sarah's voice. As she spoke, the mist swirled, then vanished as suddenly as it had come. Above them, the stars shone bright again.

The sleigh rested now in a snow-covered square, in front of a pretty red-roofed house. All about the square were tiny cottages, their windows aglow with light.

Elves surrounded the sleigh. "Who *are* these people?" . . . "Is it true, what we've heard?" . . . "Ask Sarah! She'll know!"

The Lambchops smiled and waved. The elves seemed much like ordinary men and women, except that they had pointy ears, very wrinkled faces, and were only about half as tall as Arthur. All wore leather breeches or skirts with wide pockets from which tools and needles stuck out.

"Miss Sarah!" came a voice. "Is it true? He won't go this year?"

Sarah hesitated. "Well, sort of . . . But perhaps the Lambchops here . . . Be patient. Go home, please!"

The elves straggled off toward their cottages, grumbling. "Not going?" . . . "Hah! After all our work?" . . . "The *Who*chops?" . . . "I'd go work somewhere else, but *where*?"

A plump lady in an apron bustled out of

the red-roofed house.
"Sarah! Are you all right?
Going off like that! Though
we did find your note.

Gracious! Are those *all* Lambchops, dear?"

"I'm fine, Momma!" said Sarah. "They wouldn't let Stanley come by himself. That's Stanley, there. The other one's Arthur. Stanley *was* flat, but he got round again."

"Clever!" said Mrs. Christmas. "Well! Do all come in! Are you fond of hot chocolate?"

". . . an excellent plan, I do see that. But— Oh, he's in *such* a state! And with Stanley no longer flat . . ." Mrs. Christmas sighed. "More chocolate, Lambchops? I add a dash of cinnamon. Tasty, yes?"

"Delicious," said Mrs. Lambchop.

Everyone sat silent, sipping.

Mr. Lambchop felt the time had come. "May we see him now, Mrs. Christmas? We should be getting home. So much to do, this time of year."

"You forget where you are, George," said Mrs. Lambchop. "Mrs. Christmas, surely, is aware of the demands of the season."

"I'm sorry about not being flat," Stanley said. "I did get tired of it, though."

"No need to apologize," said Mrs. Christmas. "Flat, round, whatever, people must be what shape they wish."

"So true," said Mrs. Lambchop. "But

will your husband agree?"

"We shall see. Come." Mrs. Christmas rose, and the Lambchops followed her down the hall.

Mrs. Christmas knocked on a door. "Visitors, dear! From America."

"Send 'em back!" said a deep voice.

"Sir?" Mr. Lambchop tried to sound cheerful. "A few minutes, perhaps? ''Tis the season to be jolly,' eh? We—"

"Bah!" said the voice. "Go home!"

"What a terrible temper!" Stanley said. "He doesn't want to meet us at all!"

"I already *have* met him once," Arthur whispered. "In a department store."

"That wasn't the real one, dear," Mrs. Lambchop said.

"Too bad," said Arthur. "He was much nicer than this one."

Sarah stepped forward. "Poppa? Can you hear me, Poppa?"

"I hear you, all right!" said the deep voice. "Took the Great Sleigh without permission, didn't you? Rascal!"

"The letter on your wall, Poppa?" Sarah said. "The Lambchop letter? Well, they're *here*, the whole family! It wasn't easy, Poppa! I went down their chimney and scraped my knee, and then I banged it, the *same* knee, when I—"

"SARAH!" said the voice.

Sarah hushed, and so did everyone else.

"The flat boy, eh?" said the voice. "Hmmmm . . ."

Mrs. Lambchop took a comb from her bag and tidied Arthur's hair. Mr. Lambchop straightened Stanley's collar.

"Come in!" said the voice behind the door.

4

Sarah's Father

The room was very dark, but it was possible to make out a desk at the far side, and someone seated behind it.

The Lambchops held their breaths. This was perhaps the most famous person in the world!

"Guess what, Poppa?" said Sarah, sounding quite nervous. "The

Lambchops know *names* for our reindeer!"

No answer came.

"Names, Poppa, not just *numbers*! There's Dashes and Frances and—"

"Dasher," said Stanley, "then Dancer, then—"

"*Then* Frances!" cried Sarah. "Or is it *Prances*? Then—"

"Waste of time, this!" said the figure behind the desk. But then a switch clicked, and lights came on.

The Lambchops stared.

Except for a large TV in one corner and a speaker-box on the desk, the room was much like Mr. Lambchop's study at home. There were bookshelves and comfortable chairs. Framed letters, one of them Stanley's, hung behind the desk, along with photographs of Mrs. Christmas, Sarah, and elves and reindeer, singly and in groups.

Sarah's father was large and stout, but otherwise not what they had expected.

He wore a blue zip jacket with "N. Pole Athletic Club" lettered across it, and sat with his feet, in fuzzy brown slippers, up on the desk. His long white hair and beard were in need of trimming, and the beard had crumbs in it. On the desk, along with his feet, were a plate of cookies, a bowl of potato chips, and a bottle of strawberry soda with a straw in it.

"George Lambchop, sir," said Mr. Lambchop. "Good evening. May I present my wife, Harriet, and our sons, Stanley and Arthur?"

"How do you do." Sarah's father sipped his soda. "Whichever is Stanley, step forward, please, and turn about."

Stanley stepped forward and turned about.

"You're *round*, boy!"

"I blew him up," said Arthur. "With a bicycle pump."

Sarah's father raised his eyebrows. "Very funny. Very funny indeed." He ate some potato chips. "Well? What brings you all here?"

Mr. Lambchop cleared his throat. "I understand, Mr.— No, that can't be right. What *is* the proper form of address?"

"Depends where you're from. 'Santa'

is the American way. But I'm known also as Father Christmas, *Père Noel, Babbo Natale, Julenisse* . . . Little country, way off somewhere, they call me 'The Great Hugga Wagoo.'"

"Hugga Wagoo?" Arthur laughed loudly, and Mrs. Lambchop shook her head at him.

Mr. Lambchop continued. "We understand, sir—*Santa,* if I may?—that you propose not to make your rounds this year. We are here to ask that you reconsider."

"Reconsider?" said Sarah's father. "The way things are these days? Hah! See for yourselves!"

The big TV in the corner clicked

on, and he switched from channel to channel.

The first channel showed battleships firing flaming missiles; the second, airplanes dropping bombs; the third, cars crashing other cars. Then came buildings burning, people begging for food, people hitting each other, people firing pistols at policemen. The last channel showed a game show, men and women in chicken costumes grabbing for prizes in a pool of mud.

Sarah's father switched off the TV. "Peace on Earth? Goodwill toward men? Been wasting my time, it seems!"

"You have been watching *far* too

much television," said Mrs. Lambchop. "No wonder you take a dim view of things."

"Facts are facts, madam! Everywhere, violence and greed! Hah! Right here in my own office, a whole family come begging for Christmas treats!"

The Lambchops were deeply shocked.

"I'm greedy sometimes," said Stanley. "But not always."

"I'm quite nice, actually," Arthur said. "And Stanley's even nicer than me."

"*I*, dear," said Mrs. Lambchop. "Nicer than *I*."

Mr. Lambchop, finding it hard to

believe that he was at the North Pole having a conversation like this, chose his words with care.

"You misjudge us, sir," he said. "There is indeed much violence in the world, and selfishness. But not everyone—we Lambchops, for example—"

"Hah! Different, are you?" Sarah's

father spoke into the little box on his desk. "Yo! Elf Ewald?"

"Central Files," said a voice from the box. "Ewald here."

"Ewald," said Sarah's father. "Check this year's letters, under 'U.S.A.' Bring me the 'Lambchop' file."

5

The Letters

Elf Ewald had come and gone, leaving behind a large brown folder.

"Not greedy, Lambchops? We shall see!" Sarah's father drew a letter from the folder and read it aloud.

" 'Dear Santa, My parents say I can't have a real car until I'm grown up. I want one now. A big red one. Make that

two cars, both red.' Hah! Hear that? Shameful!"

Mrs. Lambchop shook her head. "I should be interested," she said, "to learn who wrote that letter?"

"It is signed—hmmmm . . . Frederic. Frederic Lampop."

Stanley laughed. "Our name's not 'Lampop!' And we don't even know any Frederics!"

"Mistakes *do* happen, you know! I get *millions* of letters!" Sarah's father drew from the folder again. "Ah! This one's from *you*!"

"'Dear Santa,' he read. 'I hope you are fine. I need lots of gifts this year. Shoes and socks and shirts and pants and underwear. And big tents. At least a hundred of each would be nice—' A hundred! *There's* greediness!"

"It does seem a bit much, Stanley," said Mr. Lambchop. "And why tents, for goodness sake?"

"You'll see," said Stanley.

Sarah's father read on. " '. . . of each would be nice. But not delivered to my house. It was on TV about a terrible earthquake in South America where all the houses fell down, and people lost all their clothes and don't have anywhere to live. Please take everything to where the earthquake was. Thank you. Your friend, Stanley Lambchop. P.S. I would send my old clothes, but they are mostly from when I was flat and wouldn't fit anybody else.' "

"Good for you, Stanley!" said Mrs. Lambchop. "A fine idea, the tents."

"Hmmph! One letter, that's all." Sarah's father chose another letter. "This one's got jam on it."

"Excuse me," said Arthur. "I was eating a sandwich."

" 'Dear Santa,' Sarah's father read, 'I have hung up a pillowcase instead of a stocking—' Hah! The old pillowcase trick!"

"Wait!" cried Arthur. "Read the rest!"

" '. . . instead of a stocking. Please fill this up with chocolate bars, my favorite kind with nuts. My brother, Stanley, is writing to you about an earthquake, and how people there need clothes and tents and things. Well, I think they need food too, and little stoves to cook on.

So please give them the chocolate bars, and food and stoves. The bars should be the big kind. It doesn't matter about the nuts. Sincerely, Arthur Lambchop.' "

Mrs. Lambchop gave Arthur a little hug.

"All right, *two* letters," said Sarah's father. "But from brothers. Count as one, really."

He took a last letter from the folder. "Nice penmanship, this one . . . Mr. and Mrs. George Lambchop! Now there's a surprise!"

"Well, why *not*?" said Mrs. Lambchop.

Mr. Lambchop said, "No harm, eh, just dropping a line?"

Their letter was read.

" 'Dear Sir: Perhaps you expect letters from children only, since as people grow older they often begin to doubt that you truly exist. But when our two sons were very small, and asked if you were real, we said "yes." And if they were to ask again now, we would not say "no." We would say that you are not real, of course, for those who do not believe in you, but very real indeed for those who *do*. Our Christmas wish is that you will never have cause to doubt that Stanley and Arthur Lambchop, and their parents, take the latter position. Sincerely, Mr. and Mrs. George Lambchop, U.S.A.' "

Sarah's father thought for a moment. "Hmmm . . . *Latter* position? Ah! *Do* believe. I see."

"See, Poppa?" said Sarah. "No greediness! Not one—"

"Fine letters, Sarah. I agree." There was sadness in the deep voice now. "But all, Sarah, from the same family that thought to deceive me with that 'flatness' story. Flat indeed!"

Mrs. Lambchop gasped. "Deceive? Oh, no!"

"Round is round, madam." Sarah's father shook his head. "The lad's shape speaks for itself."

The hearts of all the Lambchops sank within them. Their mission had failed, they thought. For millions and millions of children all over the world, a joyful holiday was lost, perhaps never to come again.

Arthur felt especially bad. It was his fault, he told himself, for thinking of that bicycle pump.

Stanley felt worst of all. If only he hadn't grown tired of being flat, hadn't let Arthur blow him round again! If only there were proof—

And then he remembered something.

"Wait!" he shouted, and stood on tiptoe to whisper in Mrs. Lambchop's ear.

"What . . . ?" she said. "I can't—the *what*? Oh! Yes! I had forgotten! Good for you, Stanley!"

Rummaging in her bag, she found

her wallet, from which she drew a photograph. She gave it to Sarah's father.

"Do keep that," she said. "We have more at home."

The snapshot had been taken by Mr. Lambchop the day after the big bulletin board fell on Stanley. It showed him, quite flat, sliding under a closed door. Only his top half was visible, smiling up at the camera. The bottom half was still behind the door.

For a long moment, as Sarah's father studied the picture, no one spoke.

"My apologies, Lambchops," he said at last. "Flat he is. *Was*, anyhow. I've half a mind to—" He sighed. "But those red cars, asking for *two*, that—"

"That was Lam*POP*!" cried Arthur. "Not—"

"Just teasing, lad!"

Sarah's father had jumped up, a great smile on his face.

"Yo, elves!" he shouted into his speaker phone. "Prepare to load gifts! Look lively! Tomorrow is Christmas Eve, you know!"

The next moments were joyful indeed.

"Thank you, thank you! . . . Hooray! . . . Hooray! . . . Hooray!" shouted Mr. and Mrs. Lambchop, and Stanley and Arthur and Sarah.

Sarah's mother kissed everyone.

Mrs. Lambchop kissed Sarah's father, and almost fainted when she realized what she had done.

Then Sarah's father asked Stanley to autograph the sliding-under-the-door picture, and when Stanley had written "All best wishes, S. Lambchop" across the picture, he pinned it to the wall.

"Blew him round, eh?" he said to Arthur. "Like to have seen that!"

He turned to Sarah. "Come, my dear! While I freshen up, teach me those reindeer names. Then I will see our visitors safely home!"

6

Going Home

A crowd of elves had gathered with Mrs. Christmas and Sarah to say good-bye. "Bless you, Lambchops!" they called. "Thank goodness you came! . . . Think if you hadn't! . . . Whew! . . . Farewell, farewell!"

In the Great Sleigh, Sarah's father took up the reins. "Ready, Lambchops?"

He made a fine appearance now, his

hair and beard combed, and wearing a smart green cloak and cap. The famous red suit, he had explained, was reserved for delivering gifts.

"Good-bye, everyone!" called Mrs. Lambchop. "We will remember you always!"

"You bet!" cried Stanley. "I'll *never* forget!"

"But you will, dear," said Mrs. Christmas. "You will *all* forget."

"Hardly." Mr. Lambchop smiled. "An evening like this does not slip one's mind."

"Poppa will see to it, actually," said Sarah. "Snow City, all of us here . . . We're supposed to be, you know, sort of a mystery. Isn't that *silly*? I mean, if—"

"Sarah!" her father said. "We must go."

The Lambchops looked up at the night sky, still bright with stars, then turned for a last sight of the little red-roofed house behind them, and of the elves' cottages about the snowy square.

"We are ready," said Mr. Lambchop.

"Good-bye, good-bye!" called Mrs. Lambchop and Stanley and Arthur.

"Good-bye, good-bye!" called the elves, waving.

The eight reindeer tossed their heads, jingling their harness bells. One bell flew off, and Stanley caught the little silver cup in his hand. Suddenly,

as before, the jingling stopped, all was silence, and the pale mist rose again about the sleigh.

Sarah's father's voice rang clear. "Come, Dasher, Dancer, Prancer, Vixen! Come, Comet, Cupid, Donder and . . . oh, whatsisname?"

"Blitzen!" Stanley called.

"Thank you. Come, Blitzen!"

The mist swirled, closing upon the sleigh.

7

Christmas

The Lambchops all remarked the next morning on how soundly they had slept, and how late. Mr. Lambchop ate breakfast in a rush.

"Will you be all day at the office, George?" Mrs. Lambchop asked. "It *is* Christmas Eve, you know."

"There is much to do," said Mr.

Lambchop. "I will be kept late, I'm afraid."

But there was little to occupy him at his office, since a practical joker had left word he would not be in. He was home by noon to join friends and family for carol singing about the neighborhood.

Mrs. Lambchop had the carolers in for hot chocolate, which was greatly admired. She had added cinnamon, she explained; the idea had just popped into her head. The carolers were all very jolly, and Frank Smith, who lived next door, made everyone laugh, the Lambchops hardest of all, by claiming he had seen reindeer on their lawn the night before.

On Christmas morning, they opened their gifts to each other, and gifts from relatives and friends. Then came a surprise for Stanley and Arthur. Mr. Lambchop had just turned on the TV news.

". . . and now a flash from South America, from where the earthquake was," the announcer was saying. "Homeless villagers here are giving thanks this morning for a tremendous supply of socks, shirts, underwear, and food. They have also received a *thousand* tents, and a *thousand* little stoves to cook on!" The screen showed a homeless villager, looking grateful.

"The tents, and the little stoves," the villager said. "Just what we need! Bless whoever sends these tents and stoves! Also the many tasty chocolate bars with nuts!"

"He's blessing *me*!" cried Stanley. "I asked for tents in my letter. But I wasn't sure it would work."

"Well, *I* wrote about stoves." Arthur said. "*And* chocolate bars. But they didn't have to have nuts."

Happy coincidences! thought Mr. and Mrs. Lambchop, smiling at each other.

Christmas dinner, shared with various aunts, uncles, and cousins, was an enormous meal of turkey, yams, and three kinds of pie. Then everyone went ice-skating in the park. By bedtime, Stanley and Arthur were more than ready for sleep.

"A fine holiday," said Mr. Lambchop, tucking Arthur in.

"Yes indeed." Mrs. Lambchop tucked in Stanley. "Pleasant dreams, boys, and— What's this?" She had found something on the table by his bed. "Why, it's a little bell! A silver bell!"

"It was in my pocket," Stanley said. "I don't know what it's from."

"Pretty. Good night, you two," said

Mrs. Lambchop, and switched off the light.

The brothers lay silent for a moment in the dark.

"Stanley . . . ?" Arthur said. "It *was* a nice holiday, don't you think?"

"*Extra* nice," said Stanley. "But why? It's as if I have something wonderful to remember, but can't think what."

"Me too. Merry Christmas, Stanley."

"Merry Christmas, Arthur," said Stanley, and soon they were both asleep.

THE END

Jeff Brown created the beloved character of Flat Stanley as a bedtime story for his sons. He has written other outrageous books about the Lambchop family, including *Flat Stanley, Stanley and the Magic Lamp, Invisible Stanley, Stanley's Christmas Adventure, Stanley in Space,* and *Stanley, Flat Again!* You can learn more about Jeff Brown and Flat Stanley at www.flatstanleybooks.com.

Macky Pamintuan is an accomplished illustrator. He lives in the Philippines with his wife, Aymone, their baby girl, Alison, and their pet Westie, Winter.

For exclusive information on your favorite authors and artists, visit www.authortracker.com.

TURN THE PAGE FOR A
SNEAK PEEK AT:

FLAT STANLEY

His Original Adventure!

by Jeff Brown

The Big Bulletin Board

Breakfast was ready.

"I will go wake the boys," Mrs. Lambchop said to her husband, George Lambchop. Just then their younger son, Arthur, called from the bedroom he shared with his brother, Stanley.

"Hey! Come and look! Hey!"

Mr. and Mrs. Lambchop were both

1

very much in favor of politeness and careful speech. "Hay is for horses, Arthur, not people," Mr. Lambchop said as they entered the bedroom. "Try to remember that."

"Excuse me," Arthur said. "But look!"

He pointed to Stanley's bed. Across it lay the enormous bulletin board that Mr. Lambchop had given the boys a Christmas ago so that they could pin up pictures and messages and maps. It had fallen, during the night, on top of Stanley.

But Stanley was not hurt. In fact, he would still have been sleeping if he had not been woken by his brother's shout.

"What's going on here?" he called out cheerfully from beneath the enormous board.

Mr. and Mrs. Lambchop hurried to lift it from the bed.

"Heavens!" said Mrs. Lambchop.

"Gosh!" said Arthur. "Stanley's flat!"

"As a pancake," said Mr. Lambchop. "Darndest thing I've ever seen."

"Let's all have breakfast," Mrs. Lambchop said. "Then Stanley and I will go see Dr. Dan and hear what he has to say."

In his office, Dr. Dan examined Stanley all over.

"How do you feel?" he asked. "Does it hurt very much?"

"I felt sort of tickly for a while after I got up," Stanley Lambchop said, "but I feel fine now."

"Well, that's mostly how it is with these cases," said Dr. Dan.

"We'll just have to keep an eye on

4

this young fellow," he said when he had finished the examination. "Sometimes we doctors, despite all our years of training and experience, can only marvel at how little we really know."

Mrs. Lambchop said she thought Stanley's clothes would have to be altered by the tailor now, so Dr. Dan told his nurse to take Stanley's measurements.

Mrs. Lambchop wrote them down.

Stanley was four feet tall, about a foot wide, and half an inch thick.